The Emperor's New Clothes

T he emperor was mad about clothes.

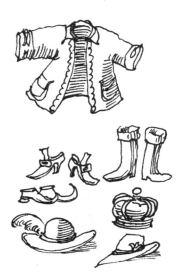

He changed his coat every time the palace clock struck the hour, his shoes every half hour and his hat every ten minutes.

In fact, the emperor was so busy dressing up in splendid outfits that he had no time for anything else.

The Emperor's New Clothes

and

The Tinder Box

Retold by Andrew Matthews

Illustrated by Peter Bailey

ORCHARD BOOKS

ORCHARD BOOKS
96 Leonard Street, London EC2A 4XD
Orchard Books Australia
14 Mars Road, Lane Cove, NSW 2066
This text was first published in Great Britain in the form
of a gift collection called *Stories from Hans Andersen*,
illustrated by Alan Snow, in 1993
This edition first published in hardback in Great Britain in 2000
First paperback publication 2001
Text © Andrew Matthews 1993
Illustrations © Peter Bailey 2000
The rights of Andrew Matthews to be identified as the author
and Peter Bailey as the illustrator of this work have
been asserted by them in accordance with the
Copyright, Designs and Patents Act, 1988.
A CIP catalogue record for this book is available from the British Library
ISBN 1 84121 661 5 (hardback)
ISBN 1 84121 663 1 (paperback)
1 3 5 7 9 10 8 6 4 2 (hardback)
1 3 5 7 9 10 8 6 4 2 (paperback)
Printed in Great Britain

"Fashions keep changing," he informed his prime minister, "and I must change to keep up with them."

One day, two strangers arrived at the palace. They said they were weavers with important news for the emperor, but they were really a pair of swindlers. When they met the emperor, they nudged one another and sniggered.

"Is something funny?" the emperor asked sternly.

"We couldn't help laughing at your clothes," the swindlers replied.

"What's wrong with my clothes?" the emperor asked anxiously.

"Out of date!" declared the swindlers. "No one wears silk shirts nowadays! And your coat might have been in fashion once, but not any more. It's lucky for you that we came along.

We can weave a cloth so beautiful it will never go out of fashion. Once you're wearing a suit made from our special cloth, you'll be the envy of every fashionable person in the world!"

These words put an excited gleam in the emperor's eyes.

"Really?" he murmured.

"There are a couple of problems, though," one of the swindlers said slyly. "The cloth is very expensive for one thing, and for another – it can't be seen by people who are stupid or who aren't doing their work properly."

"Amazing!" the emperor whispered to himself. "Not only will I be the best-dressed person on earth, but I'll be able to tell which ministers are wise and which are foolish!" He smiled at the swindlers.

"Weave me enough cloth for a new suit at once! Take as much gold from the treasury as you need."

The swindlers set up a loom in a corner of the palace and pretended to be hard at work, even though the loom was empty – unlike their pockets, which jingled with gold coins.

After a day or two, the emperor spoke to the prime minister.

"I want to know how the special cloth is coming on. You're a wise sort of chap, go and see for yourself, then report back to me."

The prime minister did as the emperor asked, but when he entered the room where the swindlers were working and saw the empty loom, he turned pale.

"I can't see a thing!" he said to himself. "I must be stupid! If the emperor finds out, I'll lose my job!"

"Well, prime minister?" smiled the swindlers. "What do you think of it?"

"Er...wonderful!" gulped the prime minister. "Such an unusual shade! Such a marvellous pattern! I can't wait to tell the emperor about it."

12

It didn't take long for news of the wonderful cloth to spread. The emperor had so many requests to view the material that when he finally saw it for himself he was surrounded by a group of very important people.

When the swindlers entered, carrying nothing, and spread nothing out like a big roll of cloth, there was complete silence. No one could see anything.

Everyone waited for someone else to speak first because they were all afraid of being thought foolish.

"Oh, magnificent!" cooed the prime minister at last. "That purple edge brings the pattern out perfectly!"

"But I can't see anything!" thought the emperor. "What if someone finds out that I'm a stupid emperor who can't do his job properly?" Out loud he said, "Marvellous!"

And at once, all the important people chattered about how beautiful the cloth looked, while the swindlers shook with silent giggles.

"In three days it will be my birthday parade," the emperor told the rogues. "I want you to make me a suit that my subjects will marvel at!"

The two rogues spent hours snipping at thin air with golden scissors and sewing nothing together with silver needles.

On the morning of the emperor's birthday, they sent him a message saying that the new clothes were ready.

The emperor arrived with two servants. The swindlers smiled broadly and held out their empty hands.

"Here are the trousers and the coat, Your Majesty," said one.

"And here is your long cloak," said the other. "If Your Majesty would take off all your clothes and stand in front of that big mirror, we shall help you to dress."

The emperor did just as the weavers said and let them move around him, making him step into the imaginary trousers and pull on the imaginary coat.

"I can hardly feel the cloth against my skin, it's so fine," said the emperor. He turned to his servants. "Hold up the edge of the cloak so that it doesn't drag on the ground," he said.

The two servants looked at the floor and frowned deeply.

"What's the matter?" asked the emperor. "Are you both too foolish to see it?"

"I've got it, Your Majesty!" cried one servant, bending down.

"So have I!" exclaimed the other.

And they both stood as though they were holding the cloak in their hands.

The swindlers left the palace faster
than dragonflies, while the emperor
went off on his parade. The streets
were packed with people, all pretending

that they were wise and could see the
emperor's clothes.

"Hurrah for the emperor!" they
shouted. "Hurrah for his new suit!"

And everybody cheered – except one little boy. He didn't know anything about the emperor's clothes.

He had been too busy playing to hear the story, and grown-ups talked about such boring things that he never listened to them anyway.

When he saw the emperor waddling along, he blushed deep red.

"There's a man with no clothes on!" he gasped.

"Hush!" said his father. "That's the emperor."

"But why hasn't he got any clothes on?" shouted the little boy.

At the sound of his shout, the cheering stopped. Whispers began to run through the crowd.

"The boy's right!"

"The emperor isn't wearing anything!"

The whispers reached the ears of the emperor, and he began to worry that they might be true.

"It can't be helped now," he told himself. "The parade must go on."

And he marched ahead more proudly than ever, followed at a distance by his ministers and the two servants, who went on holding up the cloak that wasn't there.

And that's the end of this story.

The Tinder Box

A soldier was walking smartly down the road, with a pack on his back and a sword at his side. He was on his way home from the wars. He hadn't gone far before he met an ugly old witch, whose bottom lip hung down over her chin.

"What a handsome young soldier!" the witch declared. "I'm going to give you more money than you ever dreamed of!"

"Thanks very much!" replied the soldier.

"See that big hollow tree over there?" said the witch, pointing with a warty finger. "Climb to the top and get right down inside it. I'll tie a rope to you so I can pull you back up."

"What shall I do when I'm inside?" the soldier said.

"At the bottom of the tree, you'll find a hall lit by a hundred lamps," the witch told him. "On one side of the hall are three doors. Go through the first door and you'll see a room in which there's a big wooden chest. Sitting on the chest will be a dog with eyes as big as saucers."

"Saucers?" gulped the soldier.

"Don't worry about him!" said the witch. "Take my blue apron, spread it out on the floor and pop the dog on top – then open the chest and grab as many copper coins as you can carry. Of course, if you'd rather have silver, then go into the second room. There's a dog there, too, with eyes as big as bus wheels!"

"I don't like the sound of that," said the soldier.

"Not to worry," said the witch, "put him on my apron and help yourself to the money in the chest. Of course, if

you'd rather have gold, you must go into the third room. The dog in there is enormous — with eyes as big as roundabouts — but sit him on my apron and he'll turn as cuddly as a kitten. Then you can help yourself to gold from the chest."

"What's in it for you?" the soldier asked suspiciously.

"All I want you to do is find my granny's tinder box," said the witch. "She dropped it the last time she was down there."

30

"Right you are!" said the soldier. "Tie the rope round me and give me that blue apron of yours."

The soldier climbed up the outside of the tree and lowered himself down inside it with the rope. At the bottom, he found the hall and lamps and doors just as the witch had described them.

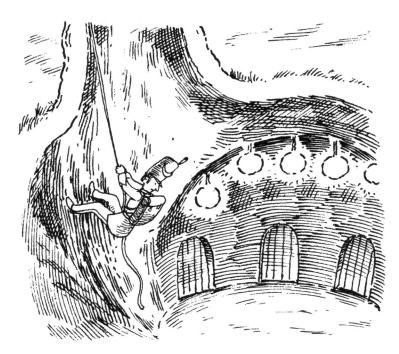

He opened the first door and saw the dog with eyes as big as saucers.

"Don't you know it's rude to stare?" said the soldier. He opened the second door – there sat the dog with eyes as big as bus wheels.

"Aye, aye!" said the soldier. "I don't like the look you're giving me!"

He opened the third door and there was the dog with eyes the size of roundabouts.

"Oh well," the soldier whispered to himself. "Nothing ventured, nothing gained!"

He spread the blue apron on the floor, lifted the dog on to it and raised the lid of the chest. There was enough gold in it to buy every toyshop and

sweetshop in the land. Quickly, the
soldier filled his pack and pockets with
gold and stuffed his boots as well. He
put the dog back on the chest, stepped
out of the room and shouted:

"Pull me up, witch!"

"Have you got the tinder box?" the witch called.

"I forgot all about it!" admitted the soldier.

He looked around until he found the tinder box lying in a corner.

The witch hauled on the rope and soon the soldier was standing on the road again.

"What's so special about this tinder box?" he asked.

"Mind your own business!" snapped the witch. "You've got your gold, now hand over the box before I cast a spell and turn you into a tadpole! In fact, I think I'll turn you into a tadpole anyway!"

"No fear!" cried the soldier.

He drew his sword and cut off the witch's head. Then he tied all his gold up in the apron, slipped the tinder box into his pocket and marched to the nearest town.

35

He took rooms in the finest inn, ordered his favourite food and bought himself smart new clothes. Because he was a rich gentleman he soon became well-known and the townspeople told him all the  latest news about the cruel king and queen and the beautiful young princess who was so good.

"I wouldn't mind seeing her!" said the soldier.

"Impossible!" came the reply. "It was predicted that she would marry a common soldier and the king won't stand for it. He keeps her locked in a copper castle behind high walls."

What with throwing parties for his new, rich friends and giving money away to the poor, the soldier found his supply of gold was soon used up. He went to live in a single room in the poor part of town where none of his new friends visited him. His fine clothes became tattered.

One dark evening when he was too poor to buy himself a candle, the soldier remembered the tinder box he had found inside the tree.

"I'm sure there's a stub of candle in it!" he thought.

He found the box and struck a bright spark off its flint. At once, the door flew open and there stood the dog with eyes like saucers, saying:

"How can I help you, master?"

"Knock me sideways, the box is magic!" muttered the soldier. To the dog, he said, "Fetch me some money, would you?"

The dog ran off and came back so fast he almost bumped into himself. In his mouth was a large bag of copper coins.

The soldier discovered that one spark from the tinder box brought the dog from the chest of copper; two sparks brought the dog from the chest of silver; three made the dog who sat on the chest of gold appear.

Now he was rich again, the soldier moved back into expensive rooms, but though all his rich friends gathered round him, he wasn't happy. He kept on thinking about the beautiful princess who was locked away.

One night, the soldier made up his mind. He struck one spark from the tinder box and up popped the dog with eyes like saucers.

"I know it's late," said the soldier, "but I have to see the princess."

Straight away, the dog was off and

back again, with the princess lying fast asleep on his back. She was so beautiful, the soldier had to give her a kiss before the dog carried her home.

Next morning at breakfast, the princess told the king and queen of the strange dream she had had about a dog and a soldier.

"I don't like the sound of that!" thought the queen.

That night, the princess's old nurse was ordered to hide in the princess's room to see whether what had happened was a dream or magic.

41

One kiss wasn't enough for the soldier. At midnight, he sent the dog again. When the dog carried off the princess, the old nurse followed as fast as she could. She saw him enter a large house and she drew a white cross on the door with a piece of chalk so she could find it again the next day.

"Now, I'm off home to bed!" she said.

When the dog took the princess back, he noticed the cross on the door, so he took a piece of chalk in his mouth and put a cross on every door in town. In the morning, when the king and queen and the nurse went searching with a company of troops, they couldn't tell which house was the right one.

But the queen was more than just a pretty face. The next night, she filled a silk bag with rice, tied it to the sleeping princess's back and cut a tiny hole in the bag so that the rice would run out and leave a trail.

At midnight, the dog came again, for by now the soldier was so in love with the princess that he wanted to marry her. The dog didn't notice the rice trail, and at dawn guards came for the soldier and flung him into a dungeon.

"You'll hang for this," one of the guards told him.

A gallows was built in the palace courtyard. The king's guards forced a large crowd of people to cheer as the king and queen sat on their tall thrones. Then the soldier was brought out.

"One last request, Your Majesty!" he cried as the rope was placed around his neck.

"Send a servant to my rooms to fetch my old pipe and tinder box – I fancy a final smoke."

The king couldn't refuse and the pipe and the tinder box were brought in a matter of minutes.

The soldier made the box spark – first once, then twice, then three times – and suddenly all the dogs were by his side.

"Help me!"
croaked the soldier.
"Stop them from
hanging me!"

The dogs rushed at
the king and queen
and the guards,
grabbed them by
the legs and noses
and threw them so
high into the air that
they never came
down again.

"Hurrah for the
soldier!" shouted
the people. "Marry
the princess and
be our king."

That's just what the soldier did. The princess was more than happy to marry the soldier of her dreams and the wedding celebrations went on for a week. And...

...the three dogs were guests of honour.